THE GHOST OF SCREWFACE HANLON

H . BEDFORD-JONES

THE GHOST OF SCREWFACE HANLON

H. BEDFORD-JONES

ILLUSTRATED BY
PETE KUHLHOFF

ALTUS PRESS • 2018

© 2018 Altus Press • First Edition—2018

PUBLISHING HISTORY

The Ghost of Screwface Hanlon originally appeared in the September 25–October 25, 1933 issues of *Short Stories* magazine.

THANKS TO

Everard P. Digges LaTouche and Gerd Pircher

TABLE OF CONTENTS

JUSTICE AND MELODRAMA

The Nephew of a King of the Underworld
Inherits His Fortune—and His Enemies.

S CREWFACE HANLON was dead!
Out across the city, through the underworld, up the river
to the Big House, spread the word. Men and women breathed
more freely. Screwface Hanlon was dead! The old miser, who
knew all the secrets of the city, had died peacefully in his sleep.

No word of it got into the newspapers. Screwface Hanlon
had long ago ceased to be news, though once he had controlled
the vice and gambling of the whole state. Only those who ceased
to tremble, knew that Screwface Hanlon had kept his grip.

Only those—and Crawford, sitting at his desk in the office
of Simons & Co., fingering the letter that told him of his uncle's
passing, of the inheritance. He was the sole heir of Screwface
Hanlon.

A girl came into the bond and brokerage office and sent in
her name to Parson Simons. Among the clerks in the outer
office passed a flutter; the Parson had luck, as usual! Crawford
lifted his head and saw her. His eyes widened. She was so slim,
so delicately slender and lovely! Yet her face held spirit—and
just now, anger.

The girl outside the rail did not see Crawford. You would
not have seen him. No one saw him, was aware of him. Nature
had given him protective coloration, and Crawford had as-
siduously cultivated it. His garments, his haircut, his speech,
were those of a million other clerks, only more so. So drab were
his features, so unmarked in any way, so devoid of expression

or outstanding traits, that if you saw him at all, you pitied his lack of character and personality. He was a cog in the machine, no more. But how he had labored to gain this effect!

Crawford was submerged, and glad of it. Once he had not been submerged. Life had been hideous. Battles on every side. Actual fights, brutal, merciless! He knew the underworld, the dark side of the city's life; he hated it, had fought his way up from it. Now he was no longer an entity. He was submerged—and dangerous.

Not a soul in this brokerage office suspected his bitter experience, his grim capability. "Puttyface," they called him. They all thought him the meek person he seemed. Never lost his temper, never showed anger. This was self-mastery, but no one suspected that it was strength instead of weakness. Strength!

A N D   N O W   he fingered the letter that ended it all. Wealth was his, inheritance, money and property; he had but to call at the lawyer's office and get what cash he might need.

"Mr. Simons will see you now, Miss Brendan. Go right in."

Crawford heard the words, looked up again. Brendan—an Irish name, eh? The fine high way she carried her head, the level look of her eyes, fascinated him. The flash of those eyes, as they met his look and went on to the door of Parson Simons' office, held anger. Yes, she was angry. A deep queer anger, hopeless, highbred—and futile enough for all that. Not the sort of anger to dent a rascal like Parson Simons!

So she went on, while Crawford read the letter again, realizing the inheritance that was now his—wealth, and with the wealth, peril closing around him.

Here in the light, airy private office, it was very quiet. The man sprawled behind the desk, straightened up a trifle as Miss Brendan entered. High-boned, well groomed, Parson Simons had a stark angular jaw, an assured, aggressive manner, a dark, steady gaze. No weakling, this! The steel-trap jaw showed what kind of man he was.

"Sit down, Miss Brendan," he said pleasantly.

"Thanks, no!" She stood slim and straight before the desk, looking him in the eyes; her look was disconcerting. "It's about those securities that belonged to my aunt, Mrs. Shannon. You remember them."

Parson Simons started slightly. "Oh! She is your aunt, you say?"

"She was. She's dead. To find everything swept away, killed her. And now, what do you mean to do about it?"

"My dear Miss Brendan, surely you can't attach any blame to me!" Parson Simons was hurt, reproachful, suave. He was frankly sincere in his regret. No flinching before a sucker!

"I assure you that I did my level best in regard to her account. For twelve years it has been my pride that the business of my clients deserves my utmost effort, and gets it! Only ten days ago, I telephoned Mrs. Shannon about those securities. I had an offer for them. I advised her to accept it, stand the temporary loss, and make it up later—"

"You lie," said the girl calmly, not lifting her voice. "Sixty thousand dollars in government bonds when it came to you. You took over those bonds yourself, replaced them with worthless securities."

"An astounding charge!" exclaimed Simons. "My dear young lady you have no proof—"

"I need none," she said, and Simons looked somewhat relieved. "No—"

She broke off and turned her head, as the door behind her was abruptly flung open. Crawford came into the private office and stood there.

"Get out of here!" snapped Parson Simons, and half rose from his chair. Miss Brendan turned to him and extended her hand.

"Sit down, you liar and thief!" she said quietly. "Sit down!"

SIMONS LOOKED up at the girl. The epithets brought a sudden dark flood of anger to his face. Both of them immediately forgot the entry of Crawford.

"You are going to listen to me," went on Miss Brendan. "You took my aunt's bonds and replaced them with Denver Rio stock, which is now worthless. You left her a pauper, you actually killed her—"

"Come! I did nothing of the sort," broke in Parson Simons. He met the attack squarely; trust him for that! "I made a mistake, yes; no more. She wanted profits, fat dividends and the stock looked good. She refused to be satisfied with government dividends, so I did the best I could for her."

"You lie," said the girl. Something terrible lay in those two calm, quiet words. They fairly stung. "What do you mean to do about it?"

"I'm going to ask you to leave this office or be ejected," Simons replied curtly.

Crawford, watching and listening, saw that the Parson knew his business, had judged this girl aright. She was not the kind to pull a gun. She had only her consuming anger; no weapons!

Nothing to fear. She had faced him with her scorn, contempt words—and this was pitifully all. These things meant nothing to Parson Simons.

"Get out!" he commanded again.

Crawford stepped forward. His movement broke in upon them both, made them aware of him, drew their eyes to him. Simons welcomed the intervention.

"Well, Crawford, what do you want?"

"To tell you something." Crawford showed no emotion, no excitement. But something in his voice vibrated queerly, attracted and held the eyes of the girl.

"I heard what this young lady said. It's true, all of it, and more! I just wanted to tell you, Parson, that I'm done. You and your crooked, doublefaced outfit, can go to hell. That's all."

A roar of anger broke from Parson Simons. He leaped to his feet, then suddenly checked himself. He saw Crawford's hand slip under his coat; but he also saw the alteration in Crawford's face, and this stupefied him. It had changed. It was not the face he knew, but a vastly different one—so filled with contempt and hatred, so charged with menace, that he dared not move.

"All right, Miss Brendan, get out while the getting's good," said Crawford.

If the girl had hoped to get anything out of Simons, she knew now the hope was futile. Without a word more, she turned and left the office. Crawford stood motionless until she had gone. Then he took his hand from under his coat. Looking at Simons, he uttered a low laugh.

With a laugh, he was gone. Nor could the infuriated Simons find him again.

CHAPTER II

AT THE curb below, as Miss Brendan stood looking for a taxicab, Crawford approached.

"My name's Crawford; you remember me, Miss Brendan. Please come down with me to Matteoni's, in the next block, and have lunch. It'll give us a place to talk, and I think we might find a talk to our mutual interest and advantage."

No flash in her eyes now. Their gray depths were cool enough, poised, but suggestive of inner hurt. She was regretting her outbreak, her words to Simons. All so useless! She had accomplished nothing. No satisfaction, after all, in telling a man what you think of him. Not that sort of a man, at least.

"Very well," she said, with a quiet nod. Then she smiled. "Did it do you any good to tell him to go to hell?"

Crawford smiled whimsically. His face leaped alive with swift humor.

"Yes, a lot," he replied. "I've wanted to do it for a long time. I've been a clerk in his office for the past year, learning things. Sixty thousand, you said? That's about what his place up the Sound cost him. Well, lunch first, talk later! Here we are."

THEY SETTLED down in a secluded booth. She found the man curiously fascinating. A clerk? Hard to say. Crawford talked a good deal, put her at her ease; the more she studied him, the more astonished she became. Yet, between them, grew a swift mutual liking. They fitted together, somehow.

"You think I'm an odd duck?" asked Crawford suddenly.

She smiled. "Yes; very. Still waters run deep, as the old adage says."

Crawford nodded. "Good. I knew right off that you had brains. You have more; something I lack. Polish. Now, let's speak frankly. Did that skunk clean you out?"

"My aunt, yes. She left me everything; it's very little."

"Let me tell you about myself, briefly." Crawford leaned back, held a match for her cigarette, met her cool and quiet eyes. He handed over the letter he had received. "First, read this. It will explain a good deal."

Her eyes dilated as she read. The legacy awaited him. The

house on Riverside Drive, with its contents; money in the bank; securities. Her gaze lifted.

"Why, you're a rich man, Mr. Crawford!"

He made a grimace. "He'd not have left it to me, only he kicked out suddenly. The man was a miser. Worse, he had been tied up with criminals. I don't imagine his money was made honestly; not that it matters! For years, until he retired, he'd been a sort of underworld boss. This was before the days of rackets and gangs. Well, now look at me!

"Gutter raised," went on Crawford. "My mother died early, my father did his best but it wasn't much good. I ran wild. I know more about crooks, about the dark places of this city, than any man alive. Oh, I've kept straight enough, myself! It was having to fight my way, raise myself above it all! But I did it. I have my own code of ethics. It may not jibe with yours. That's what I want to find out, first. Suppose all or part of your money, which the Parson legally stole—Simons, I mean; everybody calls him the Parson—suppose that money could be taken away from him. Illegally. Would you refuse to accept it?"

She had been watching him in grave appraisal. At these words, however, her laugh rang out like soft silver bells.

"Heavens, no! If some Robin Hood came along, lifted his purse, and turned it over to me—you bet I'd take it! That rascal deserves to lose it."

"He deserves more than you realize or imagine," said Crawford. "But he's not the only one. You're not the only one. Well, I'm going to claim my inheritance this afternoon; now. I must have a guard placed over that house until I get possession. Probably within a few days."

"Afraid someone will steal it?" she inquired lightly.

Crawford nodded. "What's in it. Some would like to, you bet! Screwface Hanlon knew things about a lot of people, had secrets. Maybe it's too late now, maybe not. We'll see! All that can wait. The important thing is to hit Parson Simons at once, now, this very night! It's Friday. He doesn't come to the office again till Monday. His family is in Europe. He goes to his place up the Sound this afternoon or evening, stays there. You see?"

"No, I don't." She looked at him, a slight frowning line between her brows. "What do you intend?"

"Justice," said Crawford. "Fantastic justice! Melodrama. All the trimmings you see on the stage in the movies, but never in real life. Here you'll see them! Today, tomorrow, in the future. I can get away with it. You were right about me; I can do things other men can't. But not alone! We're partners—or are we?"

She studied him for a moment, then slowly nodded.

"Yes. This one time, at least. I'll take a chance on you."

"You won't regret it." Crawford put out his hand, gripped her fingers for an instant. A sudden light leaped in his eyes, and he rose. "Then, meet me at six o'clock, here. I'll have a car—"

"I live away uptown," she put in. "If you're going up the Sound—"

"Right. Let me have your address, then. I'll pick you up at six."

H A L F   A N   hour later, Crawford was closeted with a lawyer. To his surprise, he found that Screwface Hanlon had, after all, left a will naming him as sole legatee. Had even known of his position with Simons & Co. Also, had directed a few ironic phrases at him, which the lawyer brushed aside.

"Thus the formalities are greatly simplified, Mr. Crawford," said the lawyer. "Within a few days you'll be in complete possession of the property. Until then, let me advance you whatever money you may need—"

"I've enough, thanks," said Crawford. "But we might run up and look at the house, if you have time. Is anyone in it?"

"Two guards, yes. I engaged them from a private detective agency."

Crawford grimaced. "Fire 'em, then, this afternoon. Get a couple of dicks from headquarters to live on the place until I get full possession. It can be arranged, if you pay well; so pay well and charge it to me."

"There's really nothing to prevent you moving in at once, yourself—"

"No, thanks; not today. I have other business."

The lawyer seemed to think that Hanlon's nephew was a rather queer customer.

DESPITE ITS site, there was nothing imposing about the house. It was a dingy, old-fashioned structure with a brownstone front, back from the Drive, squeezed between two huge apartment buildings. From the rickety iron gate in front, a walk led up among consumptive bushes to the house.

"Looks like the devil outside," said the lawyer, "but it's a fine old place inside."

And it was. Crawford had not been in the place for ten years, but it looked as gloomily substantial as ever. Mahogany paneling, gas lights, worn carpets and mended furniture; the home of a miser, a recluse, whose only servant had died a year previously.

Crawford passed through the rooms without comment, but paused in the library. A spacious room, this, lined high with books, an old roll-top desk in one corner, a small antique safe on rollers in another corner. The safe door sagged open. Crawford went to the desk, his eyes glinting over its disorderly piles of papers, notebooks, account books.

There! A small locked compartment on the right side. He turned to the lawyer with a question, got a shake of the head.

"I know of no keys, except the house keys. The safe was never locked, I believe."

"Then," said Crawford calmly, "turn your back for a few minutes."

With a shrug, the lawyer obeyed. Crawford produced a heavy knife with queer blades of all descriptions. He leaned forward, worked rapidly, deftly. The lock could not be picked; but it could be broken. A slight splintering sound. He opened the compartment.

A single folded paper there. He opened it, held it up, read the ironic message left by the dead man's hand:

"Ha, ha! The joke's on you, Delaney!

"The list is not destroyed, but you won't find it. Try again."

Crawford replaced the paper, with its neat copperplate writing, closed the drawer.

"No luck," he said briefly. "Let's go."

As they passed through the hall, he glanced at the stack of mail lying there on the hall table. Glanced at it carelessly, subconsciously, and passed on, talking with the lawyer about arrangements. Everything would be looked after.

THEY SEPARATED outside, the lawyer heading back downtown, Crawford across to his own lodgings. He walked, his mind busy with that message from the dead. Delaney! That must be Spike Delaney the gambler, the big shot, supposed to have a finger in every form of vice and racket. The list? What list? Well, Screwface Hanlon had been no angel. In his day, as big a man as Spike Delaney, they said.

"Something coming of all this," thought Crawford uneasily. "If he had a war on with Delaney, if he had something on the man, look out! There's trouble coming. But—oh, the devil! What a sap I was!"

He halted in swift, acute dismay. He remembered that pile of letters on the hall table, accumulated mail. Something there had caught at his attention. Now he knew of a sudden what it was. A large envelope with the others. Addressed to Hanlon; but addressed in that same copperplate writing—Hanlon's writing.

The old fox! Hanlon knew himself dying, probably, had some warning of the stroke that finished him. There usually was warning of some kind. Hanlon wanted to hide that through the mails. Safe as could be! Now it lay there with the other letters. No one would pay it the least attention.

Crawford hesitated, then went on. It was in no danger. Even if Delaney sent men to break into the place—Hanlon had expected that, evidently—they would never think of those letters. Nobody would. What was the list? Impossible to say. Might be anything. But Delaney wanted it.

Let it go, then. Safe enough, and the afternoon was drawing on. Quite a bit to do yet. A check to cash, a car to be hired, that long drive up the Sound to Simons' place. Crawford knew the place well. Twice, of a Saturday, he had been sent out from the office with important papers for Parson Simons. He knew the place and the two negro servants, and they knew him.

What would he do when he got there? Well, that was not clear yet. All depended on what would turn up; he had half a dozen half-formed schemes. The main thing was to get his belongings and leave his lodgings, take a hotel room. If Delaney was really after anything, Delaney would be on his trail in no time, perhaps was on his trail now!

Crawford chuckled softly to himself, and went his way.

CHAPTER III

CRAWFORD TOLD her all this, and more, as the light, powerful roadster hummed on its way. She questioned him, now and again. He held back nothing.

"But you don't want to mix up with this sort of people!" she exclaimed. "Why not give the list, whatever it may be, to this Delaney? Why not go to the police?"

"Miss Brendan, it's something big—big!" he said quietly. "I can fight Delaney. I don't know him, but I know a lot of his gunmen and those who work for him and with him. Now I've got money, an income, a home; and I can fight. Don't you understand? This thing has been pitched at me, and I can't drop it. Police? Nonsense. *I'm* the one! This face of mine—but you don't realize what it means. And I'm improving on it tonight, too. All depends on what turns up. I just telephoned Simons before meeting you—the place we're going to. He's not there. He's expected later on."

"Then why go there?" she asked.

Crawford chuckled. "Be there when he comes. The servants know me for a clerk from his office. Just two negroes. I'll leave you with the car; get some supper, then come back and be waiting. The getaway is the big thing."

She was silent a moment. Then:

"I don't like it! I agreed, yes; but—well, I'm afraid. Suppose you killed him or—"

Crawford broke into a low, assured laugh. "No danger! The Parson is a gambler in quite a big way, at times. He's probably gone somewhere for a game, and will show up dead broke. Perhaps drunk. He'll be easy prey for me! And you can't go back on me now."

"No. I shan't go back on you," she answered.

"I know it. But I'm not thinking just of tonight! Of all the time. You can supply all I lack, all I need." Crawford spoke softly, steadily. "If it means a fight with Delaney, if there's really something big at stake—good! You'd fit in. But a girl like you might draw back from all that. You weren't raised to it. When Delaney buys chips, there's bound to be dirty work. Killing. No knowing what! Well, think it over. This isn't any Delaney job, anyhow."

Crawford was wrong about that.

T H E   H O U S E   lay well away from the street, on a quiet, private road. A dozen houses together in a private estate, along the water's edge. Little bays indented the land, separated the properties. Crawford, having arranged a rendezvous with Mary Brendan, walked up the drive, laughed to himself at the bulge in his pockets. Melodrama! Seemed rather silly now, all his preparations.

At his ring, the veranda light was switched on. Then the door was opened. The shock was a stiff one, but his brain reacted swiftly. No use giving his name, then.

"I'm Smith, from the office," he said. "I've brought the papers for Mr. Simons to sign. The ones he had to have tonight."

The man stared at him. Negro? Not a bit of it. A gaunt-faced man, harsh of eye, gimlet of eye, deadly of eye. Yet it was the broad-voiced negro butler who had answered the telephone, an hour or so previously.

"From the office? Oh! Mr. Simons hasn't come in yet," came the response.

"He said for me to wait for him." Crawford's voice was meek. He was impersonal, quite colorless. This queer gift of switching his personality off and on at will, had never been more pronounced. The other hesitated, then swung open the door.

"Very well, of course. You can wait in the library."

Clipped accents, English intonation; a suave voice. Crawford placed it, and shrank as he stepped in. His shrinking was instinctive, no mimicry. The Duke, of course! Once before he had heard this voice. The Duke! From the stage to the gutter. A snowbird, a hophead, with two stretches up the river, many arrests, behind him. That drooping left eyelid gave the fellow away. Men told of this eyelid. Its droop marked the Duke among those in the know.

No wonder Crawford shrank. Murder was no stranger to the Duke.

"Come this way, sir. You may have to wait a bit, and it's chilly outside, eh? May I bring you a little something hot? Cook and I were just having a dram to keep out the cold. A trifle of hot punch, sir. Yes, sir. I'll have it right in."

Deference, suavity, as though the Duke had made up his mind to something and were now playing his cards. Cook and I! Sounded queer and no mistake. Queer, all of it!

Crawford sank into a chair in the library. No deep, dark room like that in Screwface Hanlon's house. A cheerful place, this; deep red curtains drawn, cheerful wicker furniture, shaded lights, cheerful pictures. The books were in alcoves, deep ones, across which more red curtains were half pulled. Seldom used, the books in this house.

Presently the Duke was back. A silver tray, a tall steaming glass, a rich aroma that warmed the room; he put it down with deference. Crawford nodded, withdrew a little into his chair, thanked him in a toneless voice. The Duke departed.

Why would a hophead, a murderer, one of the most dangerous crooks at large, be serving in Parson Simons' house? Not if the Parson knew it, certainly. Well—take a chance!

SOMEWHERE IN the house a telephone bell jingled, and again. Crawford glanced around. An instrument lay on the table, close beside the drink. He put out his hand, lifted it from the rack; a click of voices came to him. Another instrument in the house, on the same circuit. The Duke was speaking.

"A man just came from the office, sir. I really couldn't say, sir; I didn't notice his features. A clerk with papers. Yes, with the others."

"Good work." Not the voice of Simons at all! A voice instinct with authority. Curt, sharp as a whipcrack. "The Parson will be along in half an hour. He's just leaving. Is the Gaffer on the job?"

"Oh, quite, sir!" came the suave accents. "He hasn't had a drink all evening—"

"Keep his head clear, then," snapped the other. "Be sure the Parson endorses those securities. They're all negotiable; with the cash. Remember, make him open the safe! The chauffeur won't come into the house. Lives above the garage. All set?"

"All set, Spike," and the Duke laughed harshly, unaffectedly.

Crawford replaced the instrument. Spike! That would be Spike Delaney, of course. The Gaffer was here with the Duke, then; another of the same stripe. And where were the two colored servants? Where he, Crawford, would be presently. That drink!

Coincidence? Perhaps; and perhaps something more. He knew about the habits of Parson Simons. Others could know.

Simons was something of a gambler, too, and Delaney had a big thumb in every gambling pie. Crawford thrilled to it. Coincidence! No. The hand of destiny, rather. His own vague battle with Delaney somewhere in the future, thanks to his heritage; and now this, a prelude. Fate had flung them together.

The hot drink was low in the glass, grew lower still. The vase of flowers near the telephone told no tales; the aroma was rich upon the room. Crawford's head drooped on his breast, his eyes closed. His features were like a blob of putty. Drab brownish hair overhung his brow. The Duke really couldn't say what he looked like—had not noticed his features. The Duke, of all people!

"He's got it," said a voice, low and growling. That would be the Gaffer. "Where to?"

"Anywhere upstairs, and look sharp," replied the Duke. "Did you make it strong?"

"Strong enough for three of him. Sure. Better frisk him?"

"Leave him alone. He's got nothing—might look for a rod."

Hands flittered over the pockets of Crawford, a grunt of negation sounded. Then he was lifted and carried. By one man; fireman's grip. Presently dumped down on a bed, and so left. A door slammed.

He was in darkness.

Simons would be here in half an hour, eh? Or less. Crawford felt in his pockets and smiled to himself. A rod! What good was a rod to him? He had something here that was better, far better! Safer, deadlier, more silent! And he could use it.

He thought of the alcoves down there in the library, half curtained alcoves where the books rested untouched. Melodrama, eh? Nothing could be sweeter!

CHAPTER IV

THE TWO men did their work savagely, efficiently. No bungling with such hands! For all his strength, Simons was like a baby in their grip. Cruel, efficient!

Gasping, free of the noose but still purple in the face, a bandage about his eyes, he sat tied securely in the chair. He had not caught a glimpse of them, but he felt them. No slipshod, halfbaked methods here. The man was hurt, tortured; his groans died down into compliance. Huskily, he told what they wanted to know, groaned again in agony.

It was very simple. The Gaffer slid back a picture on the wall, showed the front of a safe. Simons cried out in fresh pain, and told the combination. On the table were stacked sheaves of bonds, securities, banknotes. The Duke pawed over them expertly, shoved some aside as dangerous, opened up others ready for endorsement. These he brought over to Parson Simons. The Gaffer produced a small leather bag into which he stuffed the notes, and left it ready for the other papers when signed.

The two men knotted handkerchiefs, pulled them up to their eyes. Then the Duke made ready a fountain pen and the securities. The Gaffer took the bandage from the eyes of Parson Simons, loosened his right hand.

"Sign up," said the Duke to the blinking man. "Or else—"

A low shriek of agony burst from Simons. The Gaffer knew his business. Writhing, Simons seized the pen, endorsed the certificates. They bound him again, replaced the bandage. Into the leather bag went the securities.

"Tidy up here," said the Duke in a low voice, indicating the safe and the scattered papers. "I'll lock the back doors and we'll blow."

He slipped out of the room.

The Gaffer picked up the rejected securities and papers. He went to the wall safe and stuffed them inside, then closed the safe and reached for the sliding picture. He did not see the curtains of an alcove, just at his side, move slightly. He did not see a figure emerge and stand behind him.

Clump!

The Gaffer slumped down against the wall and lay very quiet. Crawford sprang the lithe, deadly whalebone between his fingers. Such a slender thing, this life-preserver! In proper hands, better than any gun. Swift and terrible as the strike of a cobra.

Stooping, Crawford dragged the Gaffer into the alcove, darted to the table, picked up the leather bag, and dropped it in the alcove likewise. Well out of sight. Then he sat down at the table, picked up the fountain pen that still lay there, and began to write, rapidly. Fine copperplate writing. Not identical with Hanlon's, perhaps, but close enough. Delaney would not know the difference. Just a few lines:

> *"So you thought I was dead, eh? Think again, Delaney. If you want that list, come and get it yourself, and have a chat with the Ghost of Screwface."*

He folded over the paper. A step, and the Duke stood in the doorway. Stood there, staring, stupefied with amazement.

"Come in, come in," said Crawford. "Here's a note to give Delaney. The Gaffer has gone with the swag. He wouldn't wait for you."

He tossed the folded note. It curved through the air, fell at the Duke's feet. The Duke, at these words, started violently. His jaw fell, his eyes widened. And no wonder.

The figure sitting there at the table was ghastly. Yellowish, faintly luminous features, smeared over thickly as with clay; huge black-rimmed spectacles, such as old Screwface Hanlon used to wear. A skullcap atop of the head, from which protruded wisps of gray hair. Head hunched down between the shoulders.

"Who—what—who the devil are you?" demanded the Duke hoarsely.

"The Ghost of Screwface Hanlon," said Crawford, and laughed. "Heard of him, Duke? Well, shorten it down to the Ghost. Don't forget that note. Spike will want to get it. Tell him I'll be seeing him soon."

The Duke slowly stooped, not taking his gaze from Crawford, and picked up the folded paper. He thrust it into his pocket. A glitter came into his eyes.

"Screwface, eh?" he said slowly. "Well—"

It was the dope, of course. The man was hopped up, regardless of anything. The pistol leaped out in his hand. Only the glitter in those dark eyes had warned Crawford, barely in time.

His own weapon, the pistol taken from the Gaffer's pocket, had been in his hand, under the edge of the wicker table. He fired from there, without lifting the pistol. The two shots came almost as one—almost. Not quite. The Duke's bullet went wild, as he was jerked around. The weapon was dashed from his hand. His right leg crumpled and he fell forward, cursing viciously.

Crawford caught at the telephone receiver.

"Police!" he exclaimed. "Police! Help! Robbery—"

Then, leaving the instrument disconnected, he leaped to the wall switch, turned off the lights. Reaching into the alcove, he had the leather bag. A terrible cry burst from the Duke, at sight of that face in the darkness, faintly luminous, grinning, floating across the room.

Next instant, Crawford was gone to his rendezvous with Mary Brendan.

THE LIST OF DEATH

*Once More the Ghost of Screwface Hanlon Uses His
Knowledge of the Underworld to Achieve a Purpose.*

CRAWFORD LEANED forward, tense, intent, as the electric ray stabbed the darkness of the room just below him. It did not lift to the balcony. It slid forward, came to rest on the door of the library.

They had come. He knew they must come! Two days of waiting—

"All clear enough," growled a voice. "Empty. You can feel it. That's the library."

"Right," came a response. "Spike says it'll be in the library, or else upstairs in the old man's bedroom. Better split the job. You go upstairs. I'll hit the library."

A mutter of assent. Quiet steps on the old frayed carpets. The light-beam below shortened, approached the library door. Then a hoarse, humorous voice below.

"Hey, Parton! If you see Screwface Hanlon's ghost, give him my regards."

Parton, at the library door, snapped back an oath, and went on.

Crawford chuckled to himself. Screwface Hanlon had lived in this house for uncounted years, hating the world. An evil old man, linked to crime and criminals of the past. Now he was dead. Crawford, his nephew, had this heritage; money, house, and hatred. In his pocket was the list that Screwface Hanlon had left—what it was, he did not yet know. But it was something

big. Spike Delaney wanted it at any cost, and now had sent for
it.

Heritage of feud, of death! Delaney was a big man now. Ace
of the gamblers, they called him; with a finger in every underworld pie, rackets, vice, rum. Two days previously, Crawford
had blocked one of Delaney's games. Blocked it as the Ghost
of Screwface. Now he was ready to take up the feud. Not alone,
either. Mary Brendan would be awaiting him in another twenty
minutes. Time enough to do what he wanted.

How much Spike Delaney knew about him, was a question.
Spike would know of the heir, of course, but would know few
details. Crawford waited, then swung down silently from the
little balcony and came to the library door. It was slightly ajar.
Inside, the beam of light was playing over the big roll-top desk.
It halted on the locked compartment; the shadowy figure fell
to work.

Again Crawford chuckled. Inside that locked drawer was
only an ironic message that Screwface Hanlon had left there,
before he died. Parton would have it in a minute—had it now,

as the compartment came open. Crawford shoved into the room.

"It's me, Parton," he said hoarsely; take a chance, always! "No luck upstairs."

"Ain't finished here," was the response. "Here's a paper—hell! Message from old Screwface. Looks like he expected callers. Sure there was nothing upstairs?"

"Not a thing." Still imitating that hoarse voice, Crawford approached the desk. Parton began opening other drawers and compartments. As he worked, he spoke.

"Say, I forgot to tell you! Jim Masters is pulling off some big job up at Larchmont. Dunno what it is. Sparklers, most likely. The boss says for you to see him at eleven in the morning. He'll have a room at the Garvin House. You're to take the stuff off him and deliver it, while he blows out of town."

"Oke," said Crawford, and came closer. But the other straightened up, flung the light at him.

"Huh? Say, you sound funny—"

There was a thud. The light fell to the floor. Parton crumpled up. Crawford pocketed the deadly whalebone persuader, picked up the light, leaned forward. What a weapon it was for silence, for effect, if one knew how to use it!

There was the message Screwface Hanlon had left before he died, at one side. Crawford pinned it to the lapel of Parton's coat. Then he took out a rubberstamp and a pad. He was ready now, his signature prepared. He stamped the paper, then, carefully, made an impression on Parton's forehead. He threw the light on it.

Red, vivid red. A ghost with outstretched arms. What a signature! The Ghost, yes. Screwface's ghost! Spike Delaney had heard of that, before now.

Three minutes later, Crawford quietly left the house. Back from Riverside Drive, crouched in between two huge apartment buildings, the old house he had inherited. He passed out of the gate, walked to the corner, paused to light a cigarette. An officer came swinging along, and Crawford hailed him.

"Anybody live in that queer little old house between the buildings? I saw what looked to be flashlights in there, as I came by—"

"Oh, you did!" exclaimed the officer. "That's news. Thanks, buddy! I'll just take a look or so for myself."

Crawford chuckled again as he swung aboard an up-bound bus, and thought of what would happen inside his house, very shortly.

CHAPTER II

H E T O L D Mary Brendan about it, as he sat in her small apartment and fingered the envelope that contained the mysterious list She watched him, fascinated by that strange face of his—a face devoid of expression, of outstanding features, of any least thing that might click in the memory. Partly natural, partly cultivated.

Only she knew what terrible things, what unguessed possibilities, lay behind those features that few men would see and remember twice.

"So Spike Delaney knows that he's dealing with someone alive, who claims to be a ghost," concluded Crawford. "It's a battle, from now on. And before we go into my uncle's legacy, in this envelope, let's settle where you stand, Mary Brendan. Whether you chip in with me or not."

"I'm not just sure why you want me," she evaded, leaning back. Her grave, dependable eyes searched him. Delicately slim and slender, yet seeming like fine steel, she was a woman in a thousand.

"Not want. Need!" said Crawford quietly, and tapped the envelope. "I've inherited something big; what it is, I don't know yet. Haven't looked. Probably my uncle used it to blackmail Delaney. I've no illusions about old Screwface Hanlon. He was a rascal! Well, I'm not. Delaney has a finger in every big crime that's pulled off. That is, the strings all come back to him. He has gambling houses, influence—everything!"

"And you?" she asked musingly.

Crawford shrugged. "Oh, he'll be after me quick enough! Is after me now, perhaps. Well, I'm the one person able to fight him. I've been fighting for years, working my way up through the underworld; and nobody knows me. With this face, nobody remembers me. I can pull a job before a dozen witnesses, and none of them will know me again. I've worked for just that end, like a game. Everything about me the same, every detail; inconspicuous! More, I know crooks and crime. I've a wide acquaintance with people and things. I've made a study of all that! I thought once I'd be a detective, on the regular force. But not now."

"And I?" she asked. "What have I to do with all this?"

"You're the help I need," he said. "I can feel it; I know it. We fit together. I can depend on you, trust you, get advice from you. You know the side of life that's been closed to me. And we're going into it! We're heading straight into it!"

His toneless voice suddenly vibrated, leaped with hidden life.

"You don't know what's going on; I do! Not mere thuggery. Delaney is aiming high. He's no piker. He's drawing out of the little stuff. He's getting his hooks into big people, big things! Blackmail, extortion, pressure. He's wrecking people, families, right this minute. You'll read in the morning paper about something that happened tonight in Larchmont—wait and see! I'll gamble on it. I know where to reach the man who did it, and I'll reach him. Let that wait! Will you help me or not?"

She frowned a little. "It's vague. Help society against criminals? That's for novels and not for real life."

"No," said Crawford flatly. "We'll inject the book stuff into real life. Like that rubberstamp signature of mine. Melodrama! Action! Color!"

"But why?" she countered. "So much simpler to get in touch with the police, tell them what you know—"

"A stool pigeon? An informer? Bah!" Crawford gestured in contempt. "That's not playing a game, being of service, doing things! Risks? Yes. All kinds of risks, Mary Brendan! Chances to take; that's what makes it worth while! Doing things ourselves, cheating both sides, playing with them. Trust the police? Not much."

She nodded thoughtfully. "I begin to see. Well, I'll gamble with you! We'll see what shows in the morning papers, about Larchmont. If it's merely thuggery, count me out. If it's something important, something worth while—give me a ring. Agreed?"

"Agreed," he said, and drawing a deep breath, relaxed. "Agreed! And now for this legacy. At last!"

HE TURNED to the table, ripped open the envelope, and drew out several sheets of thin paper, closely typed. Mary Brendan drew up a chair beside him, peered over his shoulder as he unfolded the sheets, spread them out.

Crawford whistled slightly. That was the only sound, as they scanned this first page of typing. A list, indeed! And what a list!

"Do you get it?" asked Crawford in a low voice. "It's dynamite! And what's more, it's up to date, or fairly so. Old Screwface hadn't lost his grip! I've heard he was the big shot himself, back in the old days before rackets came to the front. He sure has kept things lined up!"

"But just what is it, exactly?" she asked. "If it's what it seems—"

"It is, and then some. People! Crooks, some of them; most of them, without any police record. Society people, business men, gold diggers, gamblers. Probably a list of Spike Delaney's officers and assistants. Every one with notations of the jobs pulled or assisted in, with addresses, with telephone numbers; why, it's inconceivable! Screwface must have been a wizard!

Here's all the dope on the men higher up—the unknown forces of the underworld!"

"Then," she said, "shouldn't this go to the police?"

Crawford gestured impatiently. "To be filed away and forgotten? Nothing here to act on. No evidence. More than anyone else, the police dare do nothing without proof. They couldn't go into court on this. But I don't go into court! To me, this list is worth anything, anything! No wonder Spike Delaney wants it."

A sudden thought struck him. Jim Masters! The name was unknown to him. Probably Masters was not a professional crook at all. He ran down one page, then the next. An exclamation broke from him.

"Look at this! The man that crook mentioned as working at Larchmont—read it!"

She leaned forward, eagerly, to read the typed paragraph:

"MASTERS, Jim (James Ward)—Dartmouth, 192—. Lawyer. Tuxedo. Park residence until 1931. Divorced 1931. Resigned from bar account Borough investigation. Dropped from several clubs, 1931-2. Weakness: Gambling, Women. Involved in Froude swindle. Civil judgments pending unpaid debts, alimony. Retains much social influence. Planned Hardwick, Nathan, Burton jobs. Occasionally employed by Delaney in active work account shrewdness. Resides Crew Hotel, Atlantic City. Remains outside state wherever possible."

Crawford put down the list.

"The decline and fall of Jim Masters, in so many words," he commented. "Once a prominent man, and now—on the ragged edge! Apparently young, too. This is the chap who's handling something tonight for Delaney, who's to be at the Garvin House in the morning, where he hands over the loot to Delaney's messenger! Then he skips. The same principle as the dip who takes a purse, slips it to a confederate, and plays injured innocence when he's searched!"

"I still think," said the girl, "that this list should go to the police."

"All right," replied Crawford with decision. "Take it. Copy it. Send in a copy to the police, if you like! But keep the original."

"You mean it?"

"Of course." Crawford leaned back, lit a cigarette. A smile leaped in his eyes. "So that's settled. Now, I have an idea! That is, if you decide to throw in with me. You buy the Hanlon house, see? As it is, the place is no use to me or anyone. Hopelessly old-fashioned. In no time, Delaney is going to find out if I keep it and live there. Instead, you buy it; tomorrow, at once! I'll drop out of sight, so far as Delaney can learn. You remodel the house, put in electric wiring. At present, it has only gas. You've seen it?"

She nodded. "I walked past there yesterday. Poor little old house! At the bottom of a well, with those apartment buildings on either side, and back as it is from the Drive."

"Exactly. Remodel it; two apartments. You take one, I'll take the other. All that will be a complete blind to Delaney or his investigators."

"I'd love to!" Her eyes kindled for an instant. Then, "But wait and see. I'm not sure, you know! Give me a ring tomorrow morning."

"Agreed," said Crawford. "But I'm going to win. This man Masters wasn't taking part in any cheap crooked game, you'll see!"

CHAPTER III

THAT LIST! Its possibilities kept Crawford awake late that night, fired him with eagerness, with visions, with plans for the future. With this, with the money inherited from Screwface Hanlon, he was armed and equipped. Where another man might have drawn back, he was plunging forward, deliberately entering the lists against Spike Delaney.

But, when he saw the morning paper, he was suddenly sobered. Delaney was fighting back!

He was appalled by it. The rapidity of the stroke, the ghastly cold-blooded brutality of it, the shrewd daring of it, left him frozen. There was no mention of any attempt on Screwface Hanlon's house; Parton and his companion had apparently evaded that officer. But there was another story, a front page story.

The body of an unidentified woman had been picked up shortly before midnight in Central Park. She had been shot twice and apparently flung from a speeding car. And on her forehead was the rubber stamp of the Ghost.

The police had acted with marvelous skill. Within an hour, at the dead of night, they traced the rubber stamp to the shop where it was made, and gained a complete description of the unknown man for whom it had been made. Crawford's description, to a dot.

So Delaney was on the trail after all! Parton had escaped, had told his story, and here was the retort. Delaney knew all about Screwface Hanlon's heir, obviously.

"Why didn't he give the police my name?" thought Crawford. "Perhaps he did. He must know I'm at this hotel. We'll see! Lord, what a lesson for me! Now I've got to act, and act fast. I'm spotted, sure enough. They know I've got Hanlon's list. They don't want it to reach the police—"

His telephone rang. An unknown voice responded.

"Mr. Crawford? Seen the morning papers, have you?"

"Yes, and very interesting news it is," said Crawford cheerfully. "Who's speaking?"

"Mr. Delaney, a friend of your late uncle. Heard of me, have you?"

"Yes, frequently. I think you got a note from my uncle last night?"

"Yes. And you're liable to get one from me, if I tell certain parties where to find you. How about it? Do I get that list or not?"

"I guess you've got me," said Crawford meekly. "What you say goes, Mr. Delaney."

"It had better! This dime novel stuff of yours gives me a pain; you can see where it's going to land you. How soon can you be up at my room at the Ritz-Plaza with that list?"

"Not right away," said Crawford. "I'm selling my uncle's property, got to sign the papers this morning. About eleven? Or maybe a little after."

"All right," snapped Delaney. "Lord help you if you try any tricks! Room eight twenty-three. You come and get your orders, and obey 'em!"

"Yes, Mr. Delaney," said Crawford humbly, and rang off.

HE DREW a deep breath. So this was it! Everything in the open now. Delaney was frightened; that's what lay behind this swift, vicious, deadly stroke. He was in the man's power now.

Ah, the Larchmont business! Crawford turned to the newspaper, scanned it, found what he sought. No indication of anything criminal. Blaine Townsend, architect and socialite of Larchmont, had been found dead the previous evening in his luxurious apartment; an overdose of chloral. Obviously suicide. He had received an unidentified visitor in the course of the evening. Financial reverses probably the cause of his action. It was said he had recently parted with the famous Townsend emeralds, handed down in his family for generations.

Crawford went to the telephone.

"Hello! Mary Brendan? Good morning to you! Have you seen the paper?"

"Yes, unfortunately," she answered. "It's terrible!"

"Oh, never mind that front page story," he said gaily. "Discount that; it's a holdup to get the list. I mean, the Larchmont affair."

"About Townsend?" Her voice was hesitant, dubious. "That doesn't seem possible—"

"It is. Did you copy the list? Good. Make a copy for me, and give it to me with the original, please, I'll meet you in an hour; ten o'clock exactly. I take it that you're willing to plunge?"

There was momentary silence, then a quiet word. "Yes."

"Good girl! You know the Garvin House? That old hotel near Lafayette Square? Then be parked in your car across from it. If you can't find space, park the car somewhere and be afoot. At ten sharp. Agreed?"

"Right," she answered.

Crawford dressed rapidly. Not a minute to lose now; a lot to do. Jim Masters had the Townsend emeralds, no doubt of it, and was expecting Delaney's emissary at eleven.

In five minutes, Crawford descended to the lobby of his hotel. Inconspicuous in garb and feature; nothing to make him stand out. One of ten thousand clerks. Utterly drab in every way. Still, they had spotted him. Someone must be here in the lobby now, keeping an eye out for him.

He went to the desk, asked for mail, got none. Paid his bill, paid a week in advance. Then back to the elevator, up to his room again, locked the door.

Now he fell swiftly and savagely to work. Here was the moment he had foreseen, against which he had prepared. Everything hung on this moment, on his success or failure! The meek, inconspicuous, unassuming Crawford was dead now. Had been killed last night.

THE CAREFULLY purchased clothes came out. Bright, modish tweeds, loosely cut, thus changing his whole appearance; linen, hose, everything, to match. Now the shoes specially constructed to give him height. What a change this detail made! No makeup; that was folly, in daylight. Not needed, either. In the glass, his drab features suddenly leaped with character, with personality. The colorless eyebrows and lids became black, thick black. Just the one thing, but it changed the man more definitely than all else put together.

Lastly, the wadded cotton inside his under lip, against the teeth. It would stay there securely. Now the indefinite features were changed. The lower lip bulged, protruded, and the change was complete. Looking in the glass, Crawford knew himself no longer. The natty soft felt hat, slightly cocked to one side—ah! And the ebony stick, the final touch, after the light overcoat and gloves.

"Putty-face Crawford, eh?" he murmured, looking into the mirror. "That's what the Fifteenth Street gang used to call you. Well, you have the advantage there, anyhow! You and your putty face! Get busy."

The built-up shoes changed his natural gait. He walked through the lobby, a natty young fellow almost too-well dressed. Not by any stretch of the imagination could he be identified with the drab Crawford. That name, that identity, was put behind him. In his pockets were everything he needed to carry away.

On the way downtown, he stopped and purchased a large crimson envelope at a stationery shop. Inside this he placed a blank sheet of paper, stamped in red with the seal of the Ghost; no writing. Sealing the envelope, he addressed it to J. W. Masters, at the Garvin House. Then he resumed his way, whistling blithely. Fight now, fight! No quarter—and no false moves. He knew what the Garvin House lobby was like.

Mary Brendan did not know him, when he pulled open the door of the roadster in which she sat. She half started up, indignantly ordering him away.

"Look again!" he said with a chuckle, and got in. She relaxed on the cushions, and stared at him in the utmost astonishment. "So you do know me, after all, eh? Meet John Carson, Esq., your new partner. Crawford has gone on a long journey."

She smiled suddenly, then became grave.

"It's wonderful!" she said. "But what about that story? That woman?"

"Delaney is a quick thinker," he said soberly, and told her of the telephone call. "See him? Yes. I'll give him the original of the list. You copied it?"

She nodded. "And sent one copy to the police commissioner."

"Who'll make a three days wonder of it, then bury it," and Carson—as he now was—laughed lightly. "Well, there's no time to waste. Delaney's messenger is due at eleven. I want to reach Masters well before then. And I can't afford to ask for him at the desk or do anything foolish. Take this, please," and he gave her the large crimson envelope. "Go into the hotel and leave this at the desk. Then clear out and wait for me here."

Her eyes searched him for a moment.

"You think—he killed Townsend?"

"Or caused the suicide, yes; and that he has the Townsend emeralds."

Without speaking, as though far from satisfied yet not trusting herself to discuss the matter further, she opened the car door and departed.

Carson waited until he saw her enter the hotel. Then he, too, left the car. As he started up the steps, she emerged, passed him with an almost imperceptible nod, and he strode on into the old hostelry.

He approached the desk without pause. There behind it was the key and mail rack. One glance showed him that the crimson envelope was in a pigeonhole; that of Room Three Forty. He went on, swinging his stick, to the elevators. The lobby was fairly well filled. Undoubtedly at least one of these persons, he thought, was a lookout for Masters, or perhaps for Delaney. If Putty-face Crawford had come in here—whew!

No one paid the least attention to him. He knew his way around. Good idea, that! Besides being a little kick-back when

Delaney got what was in the envelope. That would be later in the day, of course.

The elevator swallowed him up. Third floor. No floor clerks in this ancient hostelry. Then he was at Three Forty, knocking rapidly.

"Well?" came the question.

"Aw, open up!" said Carson. "Want me to holler out everything?"

The door opened. Carson swaggered in as Masters stood back. A thin, drawn man, the wreck of a hail fellow well met. Well dressed. Furtive eyes.

"Who the devil are you?" demanded Masters, hesitant. Carson eyed him with a laugh.

"Who'd you expect? Parton or his pal? I'm Crawford. The boss said to get the stuff and not wait till eleven, and to tip you off that somebody's given you away."

Fear flashed in the white, unwholesome features.

"Given me away? About—about—"

"Naw, not about Townsend. That's all jake," said Carson. "About the debts. They're getting a civil warrant or something. The boss says for you to hop back to Atlantic City and do it sudden; he'll send your split over there."

All this intimate acquaintance with his affairs, the mention of Townsend, more than satisfied Masters. His face cleared.

"Right," he said briskly. "Trying to catch up on the old debts, eh? You bet I'll skip! And thank Delaney for the warning. All clear about last night, eh?"

"Apparently."

Masters had never heard of Crawford, naturally. There had been the one element of risk, and was now safely past. From a suitcase in one corner of the room, Masters produced a briefcase.

"Only five grand in cash here; I took my split of the cash," he said. "The other stuff's intact. Write me out a receipt."

"I ain't prying into it," said Carson. "I'm taking it to Spike. I'll give you a receipt for the briefcase—how's that?"

Masters nodded. Carson went to the writing desk by the window, sat down with his back to the man. On a scrap of paper bearing the scarlet stamp of the Ghost, he wrote a curt receipt, then handed it over, watching Masters narrowly.

"What's this rubber stamp?" asked Masters, frowning.

"My mark. Delaney knows it."

"All right. Good luck to you!"

Whether or not Masters had read the morning papers, he asked no questions. A moment later Carson was on his way downstairs to rejoin Mary Brendan.

CHAPTER IV

MR. ANTHONY—ALIAS Spike—Delaney had just finished breakfast, at which he was not alone, when he received word of a caller. Belting his scarlet brocade dressing gown about him, he went into the reception room of his luxurious suite to receive the visitor.

Although his dressing gown pocket sagged heavily, Delaney gave no other indication of not being an ordinary valued citizen. He was spare, trim, in his late forties. Iron-gray hair lent his finely carven features an air of distinction. He was handsome, virile, energetic. His eye was iron-hard. The eye of an executive. Merciless, dominant.

When the door opened to admit Carson, Delaney eyed him with some astonishment.

"You're not Mr. Crawford?" he exclaimed.

"No," said Carson, producing an envelope. "No, just a friend of his. He wanted me to leave this with you, Mr. Delaney. You see, he's gone away."

Contempt flashed in the hard, keen gaze.

"Skipped out, has he?"

"Search me," said Carson, with a shrug. "He seemed sort of worked up over something. From what he said, I guess he's gone west. Is that what you wanted to get from him?"

Delaney thumbed open the envelope, glanced at the typed paper. He nodded quickly.

"This is it."

Carson turned. "O K, then."

And, with a careless nod, he was gone.

Below, in the street, he climbed into the roadster. Mary Brendan sent the car rolling away, then gave him a swift glance.

"Everything all right?"

"Absolutely. Did you find out about Townsend?"

"Yes," she said. "He was separated, not divorced. His widow lives in Larchmont now. Apparently she has little or nothing."

Carson touched the parcel on the seat between them.

"Got the brief-case wrapped up, eh? You're some quick worker," he said admiringly. "Where to now?"

"The express office. We'll send it right off to her."

"Right." He leaned back, and then broke into a silent laugh.

"What's the joke?" asked the girl. Carson chuckled.

"I was just thinking of Delaney's face—when he learns the truth!"

"It's no laughing matter," she said soberly. "That man is dangerous! He's going to move heaven and earth to get hold of you now! When he finds how you've tricked him, he's going to leave nothing undone to get you!"

"Sure, partner, sure!" Carson stretched out comfortably. "And that's the joke."

FACE TO FACE

The Ghost and Heir of a Dead Lord of the
Underworld Meets Face to Face the Man
Who at Present Aspires to that Position.

"SPIKE" DELANEY, lord of life and death in all
the city and half the state, stepped out of his big car
and surveyed the house set back from the Drive, between two
towering apartment buildings. His handsome, powerful features,
his iron-hard eyes, were intent. Two men, hands in pockets,
followed him from the car. One on either side of him, all three
entered through the open iron gate in the fence and slowly
walked toward the house.

"Screwface Hanlon lived here for thirty years and died here,"
said one of Delaney's guards. "Being fixed up, ain't it?"

Obviously it was. The old house had been remodeled into
two apartments. The debris of the work was being cleared away
now by laborers. Freshly painted, the old place looked spick
and span. A brass plate beside the door of the lower apartment
bore the words:

MARY BRENDAN
DESIGNER

"She's the woman who bought it off Crawford," murmured
Delaney. "Curtains upstairs, eh? Let's see her. I mean to get a
line on Crawford if it takes a million dollars!"

Telling his men to remain outside, Delaney walked to the
door and pressed the bell. After a moment Mary Brendan
opened the door, inquiringly. Delaney removed his hat.

"Miss Brendan? My name's Delaney. I'm interested in locating Mr. Crawford, who formerly owned this building. Can you give me any line on him?"

"Why, I understand he went West or somewhere, after I bought the property," exclaimed Mary Brendan. "Won't you come in?"

"Thanks, no." Delaney regarded her slender figure, her fine, level eyes, her quiet, poised features, with appreciation. "Is the upstairs rented?"

"Yes, Mr. Gilbert has just moved in—oh, there he is, coming up the walk now!"

"Well, that'll be all, thanks. Sorry to have bothered you," said Delaney, and turned away. He passed his two men, who fell in behind him, and strode out to meet the man coming up the walk from the Drive. A youngish man all dressed in gray. His face was queerly indeterminate, except for the eyes; these, behind thick-lensed spectacles, were enlarged until they stood out as the sole feature of the face one remembered.

"You're Mr. Gilbert?" inquired Delaney.

"Why, yes—that's my n-n-name," said Gilbert, stuttering.

"You're Mr. Harvey Gilbert of Roanoke, aren't you?"

"Oh, no! You've got the name wrong," protested Gilbert, still stuttering as he spoke. "I'm from D-D-Denver. My name's Charles William."

"Sorry! I've got the wrong Gilbert," said Delaney pleasantly, and moved on out toward his car. When he got there, he turned to one of his two men.

"Get a line on this Brendan dame," he said. "Find out all about her. We've drawn blank, but I've got a hunch she might know something. She's smart."

MEANTIME, MR. Charles William Gilbert mounted the stairs to his upper apartment. Once inside, he whipped off his spectacles, entered a closet of the living room, pressed a spring, and the back of the closet slid away. A twisting little flight of stairs was revealed. Descending these, he knocked three

times at a door below. Mary Brendan opened it, and he stepped into her studio, littered with sketches, a drawing board, and a dummy model.

"Do you know who that was?" he demanded excitedly.

She nodded. "He told me. Delaney. The great Spike Delaney?"

Crawford nodded. "And looking for me!"

"Yes. He asked about you. Well, make yourself comfortable. What does it mean?"

Crawford sank into a chair, produced a cigarette, and lit it. "Trouble. Let me think."

"Think all you like," and she smiled. "I have some tea ready. Back in a minute."

She left the room. Crawford wrinkled up his face, which made him look amazingly different, and puffed at his cigarette.

Without the thick spectacles, and in repose, this face of his was a blank. It had no memorable features or traits. "Putty-face," they had called him, back in the old gang days when he was working up from the bottom. Now he had inherited from his uncle, Hanlon, this property; with it wealth, information, and a life-and-death feud with Delaney. Old Screwface Hanlon, once a big man in the underworld, had left more than mere money to the nephew whom he despised as a weakling. Crawford was no weakling. He had proven it by blocking Delaney, defeating him, maddening him. Now Delaney was after him in earnest—but did not dream that he had just spoken with the man he sought so viciously.

Mary Brendan—well, she had decided to help, that was all. Interested in this amazing man whose blank, expressionless features concealed such tremendous character and ability, she had chosen to aid him in his self-appointed war with all that Delaney represented. Vice, gamblers, rackets—Delaney had a finger in every predatory game going! And Crawford was using himself, his brains, the money he had inherited, to fight Spike Delaney. With a girl to help him.

Mary Brendan returned with a tea-wagon, poured tea, settled into a chair, lit a cigarette, and regarded her guest and partner.

"Delaney has ability," she observed. "He's no thug."

"Naturally not." Crawford caught an afternoon newspaper from his pocket, passed it to her, and pointed to a story. Then he devoted himself to his tea for a moment.

"Good heavens!" Startled, she laid aside her cigarette. "Only this morning—"

"Delaney's a fast worker."

"But he's not connected with this!"

"Go on. Read it."

She was right. There was nothing to connect Delaney with the story.

An expensive automobile found in a byway of Central Park, close to noon. Two women lying in it, shot to death; Mrs. Sylvester Ponchon and her maid. The wealthy, eccentric widow, whose singular philanthropies were the talk of the town, had visited her bank half an hour previously, removing the famous

Ponchon pearls from safe storage in order to wear them at a charity ball that night. Also, she had drawn ten thousand in cash, intending this as her contribution to the funds of the ball. Jewels and cash were missing. So was her chauffeur, one Martin Wolfe—the obvious criminal. Police were combing the city for him.

"Well?" Mary Brendan looked up. "I knew Mrs. Ponchon. I saw her only last week—"

"A steady looking sort of man. I didn't notice him particularly. But anyone employed by her would have to be the right kind."

"Exactly! Remember, every crook in the city works for Delaney, directly or indirectly. Somebody else pulled this job, probably killed Wolfe and hid the body, so he'd get the blame, Delaney has brains, but damned little wit! Let's see your copy of the list Screwface Hanlon left behind him."

Mary Brendan rose, hurried from the room, and returned with the typed copy of that terrible legacy from Hanlon—that list and record of the principal people under the thumb of Delaney. People seldom suspected of crime, blackmailed by him. People without any police record; Delaney's helpers, officers, assistants. Names, addresses, telephone numbers, notations of the jobs pulled. The unseen underworld forces—the men and women higher up!

Crawford thumbed over the pages. An exclamation broke from him.

"Look at this! Ponchon, Agnes: Niece Mrs. Sylvester Ponchon, disinherited. Twice married, divorced. Expelled from France suspicion handling narcotics. Habitat, Miami and Palm Beach. When in city lives Corazon Apartments. Private telephone Stuyvesant 7091. Implicated Ashton affair. Works with Andy Lebrun. Socialite, Tuxedo Club."

Crawford laid down the pages.

"There you are, thanks to Screwface Hanlon! A wholly unsuspected person; disinherited, with nothing to gain from her aunt's death. She was with them in the car, and caused the car to stop at a certain spot in the Park—you see?"

"No, no!" exclaimed Mary Brendan urgently. "Impossible! No matter how low such a woman might sink, she could not be a party to such a crime. It's impossible! And you have no proof. You merely jump at conclusions—"

"Exactly. I'm no policeman. I need no proof! I make my own." Crawford frowned. "Your argument is good; just the same, I stick to my theory. Now, let's see."

HE PICKED up the telephone at his elbow and called Agnes Ponchon's number. The reply was prompt. Miss Ponchon was ill, quite ill. Her maid was speaking. Who was this?

"This," said Crawford, with a smile at Mary Brendan, "is James T. Bramwell, general manager of the King's County Insurance Company. Mrs. Ponchon took out a very large policy with us in favor of her niece some months ago—however, I had better drop around, if I may. Perhaps I could see Miss Ponchon briefly, within an hour?"

"Well—maybe," came the guarded response. "I'm expecting her secretary very soon, and you could see him about it, anyhow. Mr. Andrews could tell you whatever you want."

"Thank you," and Crawford rang off. He leaned back, lit a fresh cigarette, and chuckled.

"Andy Lebrun—now Mr. Andrews, secretary to the lady," he observed pleasantly. "A minor crook, confidence man, gigolo, who lives by his wits and blackmail. Lebrun is the rat who pulled this job. And he's to be reached only through the lady."

"Please!" Mary Brendan leaned forward earnestly. "I can't see you jump at conclusions like this, without protest! You're in a frightfully dangerous position—"

"And now we're dealing with murder," broke in Crawford. His voice held a steely note that checked her words instantly. "Those Ponchon pearls are fabulous; said to be worth a quarter of a million! It's a big stake, Mary. Nobody but Delaney would go after it in such a big way. Danger? Nonsense! My one chance of doing anything is to work fast, and work hard. You don't come into this picture—not right now, anyhow. I may have to call on you later."

"What are you going to do, then?" she asked, as Crawford came to his feet. He met her anxious eyes, and smiled.

"I'm going to call on the lady before Lebrun gets there," he responded. Next moment he was gone up the secret stairs to his own apartment. Once there, he shed his unobtrusive gray attire and fell rapidly to work. If Lebrun, he thought, were really the criminal, if Lebrun had to arrange for the disappearance of the unfortunate chauffeur, then the man might be detained longer than was expected. And Crawford wanted to be in the Ponchon apartment when Lebrun got there.

CHAPTER II

"THIS IS Mr. Bramwell—I telephoned a few moments ago—"

"Oh, yes!" The maid took the chain off the door and opened it. "Mr. Andrews hasn't come yet but Miss Ponchon wants you to wait. She'll see you herself in a few minutes."

"Thank you." Mr. Bramwell entered, doffing his derby. His features were not flabby nor over-fat, but his figure was, to say the least, plump. When he spoke, a glitter of gold teeth was visible between his very full lips. Black-rimmed spectacles, a high standing collar that came almost to his ears, loudly checked tweeds that accentuated his stoutness, combined to make him a notable figure. He set his hat on a table, patted his stomach, and peered about the luxurious apartment salon with a benevolent air.

Five minutes later, Agnes Ponchon appeared. At his first appraising glance, Crawford reconstructed his entire theory, his whole plan of campaign; he was acting purely upon intuition and guesswork, and in a flash he knew that Mary Brendan had been right. This woman had not been *particeps criminis*.

She was tall, slim, heavily blondined, in her early thirties, and wore a gorgeous negligee of pink velvet. Her features showed that she had recently suffered a terrible shock; she had even neglected makeup. However, she was keen enough upon the scent of money to see this visitor who told of an unexpected legacy. This fact was all Crawford needed to decide him. In two minutes he could discover whether his theory were correct.

"Miss Ponchon?" he said, with a bow. "Ah! Pardon me. One moment—"

He passed her and closed the door by which she had just come. Then he turned, with a smile.

"Sorry to have worked you up for nothing," he observed. "You see, things were devilish bad—I didn't dare tell the truth over the wire! Spike was being questioned—"

Her white face went even whiter. "Spike!" she murmured. "Are you—are you mad?"

"No," Crawford said, coming close to her. "I've got five hundred dollars here for you. Spike says to clear out for Florida instantly—get gone from this apartment inside of five minutes! Lebrun messed things up. Wolfe got away; he's telling his story at headquarters now. It's known that you were in the car. Understand?"

He was ready for anything, as he spoke. If anything went wrong with his bluff, if she were innocent, he must clear out quickly. She swayed, closed her eyes for an instant, caught at the wall for support—then was glaring at him like a tigress.

"You—all of you!" she burst out furiously. "Let me get my hands on that damned rat Lebrun—ah! To lie about it, make me a part of it—then turn it into murder—her murder—"

"Right! He was right!"

"Listen! Get wise to yourself!" exclaimed Crawford urgently, extending the five hundred in cash he had brought along. "Stick around here, and you're done! Otherwise, nobody will suspect you. Send your maid away, quickly! We'll plant another maid here and fix you up with an alibi. Don't stop to pack. Get into a dress and blow! There's an afternoon express for Miami— you can just about catch it! Either that, or face the music here!"

HE THOUGHT she would go to pieces on the spot. Then her lips drew shut, her distended eyes leaped with quick fear. She pulled herself together, with a frightful effort. She was in no condition to weigh his words.

"Right," she said, and snatched the money. "Give me five minutes."

She disappeared. Crawford lit a cigarette. If Lebrun arrived before she cleared out—well, it would be just too bad!

"She was in the car, acted as decoy," he reflected. "But she expected robbery, not murder. Give her credit for that! It has knocked her off her pins. My theory was correct. If she were pinched, she's the kind to tighten up, say nothing. The others would get off. Well, let her go! I'm the only one to know where she is. If the others are caught, then she can come along and let a jury decide whether prison—"

The maid appeared, hurriedly getting into a coat, carrying a big parcel under her arm, followed by the shrill voice of her mistress. One gone, at least! The door slammed. Then, at the bedroom door, Agnes Ponchon appeared, fastening up a dress.

"Here, you!" she stormed. "When do I get my split? You think this measly five hundred will last me—"

Crawford held up his hand. "It was all the cash Spike had on him when things broke. He said to go to the Biltmore when you reached Miami. He'll send you a couple of thousand tonight or tomorrow. You see, Lebrun mentioned him in front of Wolfe, like a fool—"

"Oh, that accursed Lebrun! I hope he burns for this, even if Doyle did do the actual work!" she flashed out. "Well, one minute more—"

She disappeared, swearing fluently in French. Fast work of it; now she had a hat, a fur coat, two bags. Crawford came forward, picked up the bags, and followed her out of the apartment to the elevator.

"Better tell them downstairs that you're leaving for the week end," he said, as they waited. "Atlantic City—sanitarium—shock of your aunt's death—"

She nodded. The elevator halted, the boy took the bags. Ten seconds later, she was gone. Crawford sauntered back into the apartment, amazed at his own luck. Lebrun, supposed to be her secretary, would not ask for her at the desk, but would come straight up. With a smile, Crawford picked up the telephone and gave Mary Brendan's number.

"Oh, hello!" he exclaimed cheerfully. "Just wanted to inform you, my dear Mary, that I was right! My theory, rather. You were also right, but I can't explain now. See you later."

H E H U N G up and then took a look about the place, but found nothing of the slightest interest. Opening Agnes Ponchon's writing desk, he sat down, took a sheet of her scented paper, and on it impressed the rubber stamp from his pocket— the ghost, arms outstretched, in red. Spike Delaney, and the police as well, knew this stamp for the mark of Crawford; who, however, had completely disappeared.

"The ghost of Screwface Hanlon!" murmured Crawford, when he had addressed the envelope to Delaney in feigned script. "Now, when Lebrun comes, I must throw him completely off the track—that'll be the only way to gain my ends. Doyle, eh? He was the gunman employed. That must be Hoppy Doyle, the rat who got out on parole last month. Can't make any pinch till we get the goods, either. They'll have the best legal sharpshooters in the city back of them—"

Still no sign of Lebrun. Crawford glanced at his watch—time for the afternoon news bulletin. He went to the radio in the corner, switched it on, tuned it in to the desired station. He was a trifle late for the announcement, but the voice that leaped out at him suddenly held him stupefied.

"—developments in the brutal Ponchon murder. This mark,

found impressed upon the windshield of the death car, is the same as that found in connection with the murdered and unidentified woman last month. It is said to have been used by a man named Crawford, supposedly the nephew of the late "Screwface" Hanlon. Turning to European news—"

Crawford switched off the radio, groped for a chair. A body-blow, this! Delaney had used the ghost mark once before. Now the name of Crawford was used. The war was on with a vengeance!

"Thank heaven I've got all the Crawford securities and cash in my hands!" muttered Crawford. "I'm outlawed now; the police will be after me hotfoot, but they won't locate me. So, even though I've left town, Delaney means to wipe me out! He doesn't believe I've gone. Well, I'll let him know I've not, before today's over!"

Two quick rings at the doorbell, then a key shoved into the lock. Lebrun! Crawford's brain leaped, as though set in motion by the sound. In a flash, he knew what must be done, had his plans made. No pity for Agnes Ponchon; she deserved none!

The door opened. Lebrun stepped in, closed the door, then froze at sight of Crawford. The latter waved his hand negligently.

"Come in, come in, Lebrun! Unless you prefer me to call you Andrews."

"Who the devil are you?" snapped the other. Crawford looked him over deliberately. Lebrun was lean and dark, hard-jawed, wolfish. No weakling. Not the kind to buckle under stress. Handsome, well-dressed—a bird of prey who knew his way around.

"My name is Bramwell, James T. Bramwell, counsellor at law, and at present acting for my client, Miss Ponchon. Come in, Lebrun—been waiting for you. Sorry you didn't fetch Doyle along. By the way, where is Wolfe?"

LEBRUN'S FACE became pallid, dirty gray in hue, but his black eyes narrowed.

"What are you talking about?"

"Come! My client has repented; she feels frightfully sorry for this whole affair, especially as you lied to her in the matter. She is not here. She has gone to a private retreat in the Catskills, leaving me to handle affairs for her. While her first impulse was to confide in the police, I may say that I argued her out of this. She has consented to let me talk for her."

Lebrun's eyes darted about the room. Bramwell smiled reassuringly, beamingly.

"Oh, no trap! No one hidden. No dictaphone. Draw up a chair and let's have a chat, unless you prefer talking to the police? It might be awkward, I'm afraid."

Slowly Lebrun advanced, his gaze boring into the man in the chair.

"What do you want?" he demanded in a low, tense voice.

"What we all want, my dear fellow! Money, of course. And before you leave this room. The split promised my client is far from sufficient. I have no time to waste, either. We must have twenty thousand dollars at once, or duty compels me to interview the police. You see, you made a great mistake in letting a woman of tender conscience know the details!"

Lebrun stood looking at him, quivering like a bird-dog pointing game.

"Twenty grand? It's absurd. Think I'm a walking bank?" he snarled. "Besides—what if I don't? She can't tell anything."

"No? But she was in the car, you know. Accessory before the fact? You can't prove it. And she's finished with you, Lebrun. Remember the Ashton affair?"

Lebrun started. He reached into his pocket, produced a cigarette case, selected a cigarette, and lighted it, very slowly. Then, inhaling, he met the gaze of Bramwell.

"You win," he said laconically. "I'll have to telephone for the money."

In those deep dark eyes, Bramwell read desperation; the man was making a bold play of some sort—and Bramwell could guess what it was. He could almost read the thoughts flitting behind those eyes.

"Sure," he replied, and rose from his chair. "By the way, here's a note Miss Ponchon left for Delaney. You might deliver it; personal, I believe. I'll see if I can scare up anything to drink in the icebox. Don't think of any doublecross, mind! It wouldn't get you anything except trouble."

Lebrun pocketed the note without comment, nodded to the advice, and reached for the telephone. Mr. Bramwell, whistling placidly, stepped out into the bedroom—and closed the door behind him. Then, like a flash, he was at the bedside, snatching up the extension instrument there. Just in time to catch Lebrun's first words.

"Doyle? I'm in a jam. At her apartment—listen to me, damn you! Get over here in a hurry; I need you. A bird here has got me against the wall, knows everything. She's spilled it to him. He's holding us up—get me? No, he's not listening. She's skipped out. I'll keep him busy till you get here—what? Oh, hell! Leave it in the bureau drawer! Nobody can get in without my key; it's safe there until tonight. You get here on the jump."

As Lebrun rose from the telephone, Mr. Bramwell sauntered back into the salon.

"Everything jake? Then, since you know this joint, come give me a hand. I can't find any liquor, and we ought to have a drink on it."

"Sure thing!" exclaimed Lebrun cordially. "Here's the kitchen—off this way, through the dining room. Come along. Know Delaney, do you?"

"Distantly," and Mr. Bramwell chuckled. "He'll know me better later on."

"Well, that's your funeral," was Lebrun's pleasant comment as he swung open the door of the kitchen. "The money will be here in no time. Now for the ice box!"

"Ginger ale, if there is any," suggested Mr. Bramwell.

Lebrun complied, handing out two bottles, then reaching

for a bottle of gin next the ice. An unfortunate reach for him. Bramwell was already swinging one of the ginger ale bottles. It hit Lebrun on the back of the skull and the man collapsed, senseless, without knowing what hit him.

Mr. Bramwell pounced upon him with dishtowels, tied him up, searched him. A letter, sure enough, addressed to Lebrun—giving his address. With this, Mr. Bramwell went to the telephone and called police headquarters.

"Homicide squad, please—ah! Hello! Here's some dope for you on the Ponchon murder, Sergeant. It was done by Andy Lebrun and Hoppy Doyle; Doyle did the killing. The pearls, and probably the money, are in a bureau drawer in Lebrun's apartment—here's the address," and Bramwell read it off. "Lebrun is now in Apartment Eighteen, the Corazon. It is the apartment of Agnes Ponchon, niece of the murdered woman. Agnes helped with the job, but didn't know it involved murder. She caught the afternoon Miami express; better have her taken off at Atlantic City. Rush some men to the Corazon or you'll lose Lebrun. You may get Doyle there also, if you hurry."

Regardless of the frantic, explosive voice on the line, Mr. Bramwell hung up, and smiled happily.

"I think that is all," he murmured, glancing around. "They'll be nabbed, the loot will be found—and one of the three will talk to keep from burning! And Mr. Spike Delaney will discover that it wasn't wise to try to frame the ghost of Screwface Hanlon! All in all, a very neat job."

Picking up his hat—which was marked with his correct initials—Mr. Bramwell put it on his head, threw a last glance about the room, then started for the door. He put out his hand to it—

"Up!" crackled a voice behind him. "Up, blast you!"

CHAPTER III

I N   T H E   kitchen doorway stood Hoppy Doyle, pistol in hand. He must have come up to the apartment by the back way.

Crawford recognized him instantly from his pictures, though he had never met the man. His hands went up. Doyle advanced tigerishly, a blaze of suspicion and anger in his face.

"So you're the guy, are you? What's the idea, leaving Lebrun in the kitchen that way? And what's it all about? Just walking out, were you? Come back here."

Crawford obeyed. Doyle had seen the prone figure of Lebrun, had swept silently on into the salon—but as yet knew little. Still a chance! Desperation spurring at him, Crawford mentally cursed his folly in lingering here, even as he spoke.

"What is this—are you a burglar? What are you doing with that gun?"

Doyle glared at him. "Come here!" The pistol jabbed into Crawford; a hand frisked him rapidly, found no weapon. "Get out into the kitchen—step! Laid him out, did you?"

Crawford backed into the kitchen. He was caught now in his own trap, sought frantically for some way of escape, found none. A glance at the figure of Lebrun—the latter's eyes were open. He spoke feebly.

"Hoppy! Help me—get that bird—get him first! Damn him—"

Doyle whirled about. Deadly purpose in his face, in his attitude. No foolery here; the killer meant to finish the job—

Crawford leaped at him. The pistol roared; the two men collided, grappled, went reeling across the kitchen. Life and death now—Doyle fought savagely, but he was no match for the terrific energy that blazed in Crawford. The pistol exploded again. The two stumbled into the twisting, writhing Lebrun, went crashing down across his body.

Doyle's head was split against the open door of the refrigerator.

After a minute, Crawford came dizzily to his feet. Doyle was not the kind to miss; he had not missed. Nothing in sight outwardly. With an effort, Crawford picked up his hat and staggered out of the room. No hesitation now. Across to the apartment door, out into the hall. Somehow, he must make it—he must!

He came to the elevator, rang, waited. Down the hall ran a man, then another; they paid no heed to the figure leaning against the wall by the elevator. Shooting! Someone shot! Crawford heard their voices dimly. The elevator door clanged open.

He stepped out into the lobby, walked steadily to the entrance. A taxicab was under the canopy; Crawford signaled it. As he stepped in, the long blast of a siren came down the street. A police car.

Agony seized him. He fell back on the cushions, gasped out his address, felt the hot blood soaking his clothes. Not far to go, luckily. When the taxicab stopped, he leaned forward.

"You'll have to give me a hand in," he said. "Heart seizure—"

The sympathetic driver took his arm, supported him. The door of Mary Brendan's lower apartment opened. Spike Delaney came out, strode up the walk.

"Hello!" he exclaimed. "Somebody; hurt?"

Crawford adjusted his black-rimmed spectacles. "No, thanks," he responded. "A bad heart—can you tell me if my friend Mr. Gilbert lives here? I think this is his new address. Charles W. Gilbert."

"Upstairs flat," said Delaney, and swung on. Crawford chuckled. Face to face—and Delaney had not recognized him! That was a triumph.

Five minutes later he was in a chair upstairs. A tap at the secret door. Mary Brendan appeared, white-faced, anxious.

"What is it? You're hurt—"

"More or less. What did Delaney want?"

"Oh, nothing. He's sending me some designing—invited me out to dinner," she said impatiently. "Tell me! What's wrong! Where are you hurt?"

Crawford heard her voice die away. When he opened his eyes, he was stripped to the waist, bandaged, stiff. She stood looking down at him, stormy-eyed.

"Do you know you nearly bled to death? A bullet went between your arm and your side, not two inches from your heart—gouged across your ribs—"

Crawford laughed suddenly.

"Invited you out to dinner, did he? Confound his nerve! Well, he'll have other things to busy himself with. The police have got the right ones this time, Mary—got 'em cold! Only loss of blood, eh? And Delaney came face to face with me and never knew me—"

"It's no laughing matter!" she exclaimed angrily.

"But it is!" retorted Crawford, thinking of the note in Lebrun's pocket—the note addressed to Delaney. "If you only knew!"

ABOUT THE AUTHOR

H. BEDFORD-JONES is a Canadian by birth, but not by profession, having removed to the United States at the age of one year. For over twenty years he has been more or less profitably engaged in writing and traveling. As he has seldom resided in one place longer than a year or so and is a person of retiring habits, he is somewhat a man of mystery; more than once he has suffered from unscrupulous gentlemen who impersonated him—one of whom murdered a wife and was subsequently shot by the police, luckily after losing his alias.

The real Bedford-Jones is an elderly man, whose gray hair and precise attire give him rather the appearance of a retired foreign diplomat. His hobby is stamp collecting, and his collection of Japan is said to be one of the finest in existence. At present writing he is en route to Morocco, and when this appears in print he will probably be somewhere on the Mojave Desert in company with Erle Stanley Gardner.

Questioned as to the main facts in his life, he declared there was only one main fact, but it was not for publication; that his life had been uneventful except for numerous financial losses, and that his only adventures lay in evading adventurers. In his younger years he was something of an athlete, but the encroachments of age preclude any active pursuits except that of motoring. He is usually to be found poring over his stamps, working at his typewriter, or laboring in his California rose garden, which is one of the sights of Cathedral Cañon, near Palm Springs.